This book
belongs
to

_____

Young Readers Book Club presents…

WILLY BEAR

By Mildred Kantrowitz

Illustrated by Nancy Winslow Parker

ALADDIN BOOKS

MACMILLAN PUBLISHING COMPANY · NEW YORK
COLLIER MACMILLAN PUBLISHERS · LONDON

Text copyright © 1976 by Mildred Kantrowitz
Illustrations copyright © 1976 by Nancy Winslow Parker

Aladdin Books
Macmillan Publishing Company
866 Third Avenue, New York, NY 10022
Collier Macmillan Canada, Inc.

First Aladdin Books edition 1989
Printed in the United States of America

A B C D   0 1 2 3

Library of Congress Cataloging-in-Publication Data
Kantrowitz, Mildred
Willy Bear/by Mildred Kantrowitz; illustrated by Nancy Winslow
Parker.—1st Aladdin Books ed.
*   p.   cm.*
Summary: On the eve of his first day at school, a child projects some of
his uneasiness onto his teddy bear, Willy.
ISBN 0-689-71345-2
{1. Schools—Fiction.   2. Nights—Fiction.
3. Teddy bears—Fiction.}   I. Parker, Nancy Winslow, ill.
II. Title.
{PZ7.K1285Wi 1989}
{E}—dc19   89-31868   CIP   AC

To Beginnings

Good-night, Willy.
Close your eyes and go right to sleep.
I kiss you on the tip of your nose.
Just like always.
And when you get up in the morning
I want you to be bright and cheerful,
not cranky. Do you know why?

Tomorrow you are going to school.

School is a very nice place to go.
You have to be big enough, and old enough,
and grown up enough. Just like you.

Now I will kiss you on your toes
and on your ears.
Good-night, Willy Bear.

Willy?
Are you sleeping?
Are you still awake?
Is it too dark in the room?

Now that you
are all grown up
I put out the lights.

I know you're not afraid of the dark!
But would one small light make you feel better?
O.K. Just tonight. There . . .
I feel better too.

Good-night, Willy Bear.

Willy?

Are you still awake?

I can see from my bed that your eyes are wide open.

Why can't you fall asleep?

I know the reason. You're thirsty!

Sometimes when you're very thirsty you can't go to sleep.

I will get you a glass of water.

Now drink it slowly.
May I have some?

M-m-m . . . I was thirsty, too.
I feel much better. Don't you?

Good-night, Willy Bear.

Willy?
You're not still awake, are you?
I know what the problem is.

I think that you would like to come over
and snuggle next to me on my soft pillow,
like we always did.
Just because you're all grown up
doesn't mean you can't snuggle anymore.
We're still friends, aren't we?

You feel so nice and soft.

Good-night, Willy Bear.

Willy...?   Where are you!

Oh, there you are. On the floor.

Have you brushed your teeth?

Did you wash your face?

Have you eaten your breakfast?

YOU'RE NOT EVEN DRESSED YET!

Well, I will just have to leave without you.

Oh, Willy Bear, don't look so sad. I still love you.
I always will. If you really want to know,
I'm doing all this just for you. I will go to school first,

and I will meet YOUR new teacher.
I will taste YOUR milk and cookies,
and I will meet YOUR new friends.

Then I will come right home, and
I'll tell you all about it.
Now you sit here at the window where
you can watch me leave. I will wave.
You're very brave, Willy.
You are all grown up!

Good-bye, Willy Bear.